Detective Willow Fae
Mrs Magpie's Dilemma

Written and illustrated by
Debra O'Halloran

"Ah! This is the life." Willow Fae said to herself as she lay back in the hammock while it rocked gently in the breeze. She could quite easily get used to not having to solve a problem, even for one hour, but there's always a problem somewhere that needs to be solved. She closed her eyes, listening to the trees whispering amongst themselves, as the warm sun kissed her cheeks making her very sleepy.

Detective Willow Fae of the Tree Clan is famous amongst all wildlife and Clans from many Realms. She is the youngest daughter of King Faidae, the ruler of all mystical beings in the province. The Fae Clan has ruled since the beginning of time and is respected by all.

Willow is of a caring nature and has always tried to assist others wherever she can and this is how her title as Detective came about because she made it her mission to help others in a crisis. She has solved many cases, from Father Time losing his second hand to helping Lizzie the lizard find her tail. Her latest case was to recover the rare blue-berries that Madam Sophie was collecting for a delicious pie. Madam had spent all day collecting them and was waiting for them to dry when they had disappeared. Willow had found that Mr Bower Bird was using them to attract a partner to his nest; he was very contrite about the whole thing. It's cases like this that Detective Willow Fae's famous for, because she's never ever had a case that she could not solve.

Suddenly the trees stopped whispering and a familiar voice from above called out. "Willow! Willow!"

The voice was from young Dixie, who lives' nearby with a village of Pixies. The bright green hat covering his red curly hair and the freckles across the bridge of his nose are as well known to the forest inhabitants as Willow.

"Well, that did not last long." sighed Willow to herself as she stirred from her sleep.   Willow saw Dixie peering down at her through the leaves of the tree branch above her. She saw the concern in his eyes, so she climbed out of the hammock and flew up to him. "Hello Dixie, what has you looking so worried?"

Dixie blurted out excitedly. "Its Mrs Magpie, she is flappin' and squawkin' and pacin' the branch of her tree. When I ask her what is the matter she doesn't seem to hear me. She just continues to look into the nest, shake her head and begin pacin' again. I'm worried somethin' has happin' to one of her eggs. You see she just laid four eggs last week. She was so proud that she was callin' out to anyone that passed by and tellin' em."

"Mmm, I see" said Willow to Dixie "You know Dixie, that does sound quite serious; I had better go and speak to Mrs Magpie." She stopped and pondered for a moment, looking at Dixie, she said, "You know Dixie, I may need some help with this one. How would you like to be my apprentice and help me solve problems?" Dixie's eyes became as big as saucers and he could barely contain himself. Willow continued "Mind you, we have to be alert at all times and look for things that may help us discover the truth. Can you do that?" Dixie nodded his head so hard, Willow was worried he was going to loose his green cap. "Oh yes, yes I will! I want to be just like you Detective Willow!" he said enthusiastically.

"**A**lright then, first of all we need to get the tools that will help us in our investigation." Willow said. "Tools?" asked Dixie, "What tools?" Wiggling her finger she said, "Come with me."

They flew down to the largest branch of the tree to the door of Willow's home, which is well hidden amongst the leaves. Dixie waited nearby while Willow disappeared inside. When she came out a few minutes later she had a brown satchel in hand. Opening it, Willow pulled out a piece of glass that made her face look huge when she put it to her eye and looked at Dixie. Dixie backed up with a start. Willow laughed and said, "This is called a peer glass, it helps me to see things that are small. Here you have a look, but be careful not to drop it." Dixie carefully put the glass to his eye and was amazed at how big things looked. He saw a small bug become as big as his foot. "Wow!" was all he could say. He carefully gave Willow the glass so she could placed it back into the bag. She said, "We also need some strong rope, a note-book and pen. Mostly, we need good minds to think wisely!" Looking confused, Dixie asked, "How do we do that?"

"By looking for little things that may be a clue, sometimes the smallest things can be missed. So, we need to ask questions that may help us work out the what, the why and the how of the problem." explained Willow. "Shall we go and see why Mrs Magpie is in such a dilemma?" Eager to get started Dixie said "Yes, lets."

Together Detective Willow and her apprentice Pixie Dixie flew to where Mrs Magpie had built her nest of twigs and feathers.

The pair came upon her still pacing and squawking frantically. Willow stood in the path of the big black and white bird to get her attention. "Mrs Magpie, what is the problem? What has happened?" Mrs Magpie stopped, peered down at Willow and Dixie and gave a very loud sorrowful bird call. All she could say was, "My babies, my babies I just don't know, I don't know," she cried, not making any sense at all to Willow or Dixie.

Willow reached up with both her hands and placed them either side of Mrs Magpie's beak and said, "Now Mrs Magpie, we cannot help you unless you calm down and tell us exactly what has happened."

Closing her eyes, Mrs Magpie seemed to control herself before she spoke. "Willow, I just don't know, I'm all a fuss, I left my four babies nesting comfortably in my magnificent nest. I went to find a worm or two before settling down to sit on them. When I came back there where FIVE eggs in the nest. Oh me! Oh my. What am I to do? They all look the same, what am I to do? Who could have put another egg in my magnificent nest? It's just not big enough for five young'uns!"

"Oh yes, I see the problem Mrs Magpie," Willow said as she looked into the nest that was overcrowded with five bluish green eggs with brown coloured markings. "Let me see through my peer glass to see if I can tell which egg might be the fake egg. Sometimes a closer look can pick up things you can't see with the naked eye." Pulling out the glass, Willow peered very closely at each egg, lifting one at a time to the sun. It seemed a very long time before she looked up and told Dixie to have a look.

Dixie looked through the glass the same way Willow had done, looking very serious He said, "Yup, there's definitely five eggs and they look all the same to me!" Willow smiled at him and said, "Do you see anything else besides the eggs Dixie? Remember we have to look for the smallest things that don't belong." Dixie looked again and said thoughtfully, "Well, the nest is made of sticks and has all sorts of feathers and leaves lining the nest, but I can't see anything out of the ordinary."

"Ok, let us have a closer look together." Willow said. All three heads looked into the nest while she pointed out what she had discovered. "These feathers here are the same type, probably from the human's chicken house, is that right Mrs Magpie?" "Why yes, because they are so soft and warm," replied Mrs Magpie. Willow nodded and said, "But this one is grey and possibly from a wing, but not yours Mrs Magpie. Do you recall getting this one?" Tilting her head to the side, Mrs Magpie said, "No, I don't it is not one that I would have picked. Where could it have come from?" Willow picked up the feather and studied it for a moment before she said, "I believe this feather was left by the bird who laid the extra egg in your nest."

"Oh my goodness, what cheek!" cried Mrs Magpie "What am I to do? When they all hatch there will not be enough room or food to feed them all. What to do, what to do!" Mrs Magpie became distressed again, pacing once more. Dixie went to Mrs Magpie and gave her a hug and reassured her that Detective Willow and her apprentice are on the case. "Isn't that right, Detective Willow?" Distractedly, Willow, already looking for more clues, said, "Yes, of course Mrs Magpie, you must trust us to discover which egg is not yours and find the parent of the bogus egg. Do not worry yourself, we will find a solution to your problem."

Willow, checked each egg and wrote notes in her battered old pocket book, listing items of interest that may help with their investigation. As she did so she pointed out details to her newly appointed apprentice. She placed a mark on the egg she believed did not belong in the nest. Willow suggested they fly down to the forest floor to see if they could find any more clues.

While searching around the base of the tree, they came upon Mrs Roo, who was resting in the shade while her baby Joey was chasing a butterfly.

"Hello Mrs Roo, how are you today?" said Willow "Oh, hello Detective Willow, are you on another case?" With an important voice, Dixie spoke up and said, "It's a terribly important case and I'm Detective Willow's apprentice." "Well, that is exciting Dixie, you will have a good teacher in Detective Willow." smiled Mrs Roo. "Hey! Can I be a-apentice too?" asked little Joey. Mrs Roo shook her head and said to Joey, "It's 'apprentice' dear, and you are too young, maybe in a year or two." Joey hung his head looking very sad. Willow Fae touched Joey on the head and said, "You know what would be really helpful Joey? If you could be my scout and keep your eyes open for any unusual activities. Do you think you can do that? It is a very important job." Joey stood tall and said, "Oh can I Mum?" looking to his Mum for approval, Mrs Roo nodded and Joey cried, "Yahoo! I will be the best scout ever Detective Willow."

"Good, very good. Now, I wanted to ask you both if you can recall any strange birds in the area over the last few days?" Willow asked them both. "No, I don't think so dear. At least not down here!" Mrs Roo said. "Not me either, Mum's kept me in the pouch cause I got a cold!" piped in Joey. "Oh that's not good Joey, you look better now though." Willow said smiling at him. "Thanks anyway, now don't forget to keep a look out and let me know if you do see anything. Well Dixie, we'd better be off." Waving goodbye, the pair flew up into the trees out of sight of the Kangaroo and Joey.

"Where are we going Detective Willow?" asked Dixie

"We are going to see someone who can identify the species of bird the feather belongs to so we will know where to look next." said Willow. "The Priestess lives just over the other side of this hill."

When they landed they were on the edge of a forest next to a big old oak tree. Dixie was about to ask what they were doing there when Willow lifted her hand and a tinkling sound rang through the air. Dixie did not know where it came from and he was even more confused when a voice called out from the forest. "Willow Fae, how lovely to see you!" said the strong male voice. "Tol-a-fae to you Guardian Alrea." said Willow. Dixie tugged on Willow's dress. "Willow? Who is there? I don't see anyone!" "Shh! Dixie be patient, you will see soon enough." whispered Willow.

Dixie heard. "What is this little mischief doing here Willow?" The voice sounded not too pleased, so Dixie dashed behind Willow, afraid of what he might do. "This is Dixie, he is my new apprentice and helping me in a case." she said to Guardian Alrea, taking Dixie's hand to guide him beside her again. "We need to see the Grand Priestess if possible?"

The Guardian said, "The Priestess is expecting you, she has already arranged a light supper for you in the garden of roses. Against my better judgment, I am to give the Pixie the sight to see, but be advised that all memory of our lands will be wiped from his mind when he leaves." Nodding agreement, Willow said, "I understand and thank you, Guardian Alrea, we will be ever so grateful."

The Guardian was satisfied, it would be safe to allow the Pixie to see the Elven City and reached into his pouch attached to his belt and blew the fine blue dust upon the Pixie.

"Ah-ah-archoo!" sneezed Dixie. When he opened his eyes, the forest began to disappear, and in its place was an archway made of stone and iron with vines cascading down the walls. Beyond the gates there was a strange glowing amber that seemed to reach the very skies. The city of white majestic structures nestled amongst the rocks, with cascading waterfalls creating rainbows everywhere.

Dixie could now see the tall Elven figure who Willow had been speaking to. The Elven's hair was bright white and long, in his hand he carried a staff that held a glowing blue crystal held in place by a band of gold. The silver band on his head signified his station as the Guardian Keeper of the Elven gates. The stern look on the Guardian's face made Dixie want to keep his distance.

The Guardian bent down, looking deeply into the Pixie's eyes and said sternly, "I am the Guardian of Elven Lands young Pixie, and it is only the word of Willow Fae that has allowed you the opportunity to visit our world.   Do not, under any circumstances stray from Willow's side, as you may find yourself in deep trouble. Understood?"

"Y-yes Sir!" stuttered Dixie, who was quite frightened of the tall figure staring down at him with cold piercing blue eyes. Dixie felt sure the Guardian would have liked to freeze him on the spot. Willow stood beside Dixie and laid her hand upon his shoulders to comfort him. She said to the Guardian "I assure you, Guardian Alrae, he will be on his very best behavior, won't you Dixie?" Unable to speak, Dixie nodded his head confirming yes. Alrea seemed to soften somewhat and said, "Very well Willow, I believe you would not bring any creature here that would do us harm. The Priestess is waiting for you. Keep to the blue path, it will take you to the garden of roses safely." said Alrea

"Thank you so much Alrea." said Willow. Dixie looked up at the Guardian and gave him his biggest smile. Unable to ignore the offer of friendship, the Guardian grinned back at Dixie as a wisp of smoke swirled around him and he disappeared before their very eyes.

Dixie asked, "Detective Willow? How come I haven't heard of this place before, and what did the Guardian blow on me?" Dixie asked

"Well Dixie, you see, the Guardians, like Alrea are the keepers and use their magical powers to hide the gates and all who live within from the outside world. The reason for this is, many centuries ago a terrible war broke out between the Elven Clans and the Netherlander Pixies. Many were killed on both sides, almost destroying the Elven lands. This is why the Guardians where appointed to hide and guard their lands." Willow explained, "The dust Alrea used to help you see is their special blend of magic which only allows you temporary sight. Once we leave you will not remember anything of this place." Seeing the concern in Dixie's eyes, Willow smiled and said, "Come along, let us follow the blue path to see the Priestess" Wide eyed and astonised by the beauty surrounding them, Dixie followed Willow closely to ensure he did not get into trouble.

The pair walked the blue path that seemed to float off the ground and was clear as glass. It meandered around the trees and over ponds until they came to a stone staircase leading into the loveliest garden Dixie had ever seen. The roses of multiple colours and sizes surrounded a stone floor, with seats placed around the edges. In the middle of the floor was a table with all sorts of cakes, biscuits and a jug of lemon water. Standing beside the table was the Priestess. She had long golden hair that lay over her shoulders and a gold band on her head. Her dress draped lightly down to her feet, giving her the appearance of floating on air.

Dixie was very shy in the presence of the Priestess, and could not stop looking at her. Her voice, when she spoke, was smooth as silk and barely a whisper. "Come along young Dixie, you have nothing to fear. I know you have a good heart and you are welcome to share in the table of food and drink." Dixie smiled and said, very politely, "Thank you Mam." Opening her arms, the Priestess invited them both to sit. They climbed upon the chairs as the Priestess waved her hand over the jug and it magically lifted off the table and poured its contents into each glass. Dixie just could not believe his eyes.

"Thank you, High Priestess, for taking the time to see us. We are investigating a case and I thought you may be able to assist us in identifying a feather that was found at the scene. We are trying to determine what bird may have left it." Willow explained, as she pulled the feather from her bag and handed it to the Priestess. After looking at the feather, the Priestess held it between her hands and closed her eyes. Her skin began to glow and a ray of gold shone around her. It was as if a light had been switched on inside her.

Dixie looked up in mid-bite, mouth and eyes wide open in surprise. He snapped his mouth shut when the Priestess looked directly at him with a gentle smile. Turning to Willow she said, "This belongs to the Channel-billed Cuckoo Bird, Willow. They are notorious for laying their eggs in the nests of others, and have developed the ability to disguise the egg with the likeness of the hosts. They leave the caring of their young to others so they can fly to warmer climate. The chicks are usually bigger than the hosts babies and will take their food and push the hosts chicks out of the nest. It is not an ideal situation, the Cuckoo Birds need to be chastised for this habit."

"Do you know where I may find the Cuckoo Bird now?" asked Willow. The High Priestess pondered for a moment and said, "As the fall is almost over and preparation for winter is upon us, the Cuckoo Bird, will be on their way to warmer lands. They will not return until six full moons have graced the skies." "Goodness, that does pose a problem." Willow sighed, "We must think of another solution to this problem.

"Look for the blue pearl and you will find a solution to what you seek." said the High Priestess very mysteriously. Willow and Dixie were not quite sure what she meant. "The answer is with the blue pearl." she said again.

"Thank you so much for your help Priestess." The Priestess bowed her head and said, "It has been lovely to see you again Willow. Dixie it has been a great pleasure to meet you, I feel you will do many great things and we will see more of you." Dixie said, "Really? Me? Wow, thanks Mam." Walking to the pathway and admiring the beautiful roses, the visitors turned to wave to the Priestess at the top of the stone staircase, but she had already disappeared.

A bright light and thick fog enveloped the visitors making them weightless. In a matter of minutes, the mist cleared and they were once again at the edge of the forest.

Dixie looked very puzzled as the memory of the last hour had been wiped from his mind. He was about to ask Willow how they got there when, suddenly, he became warm all over, and the memories came flooding back.

A gentle whisper in his ear said, "Keep our secret safe little one." Dixie looked at Willow, who just smiled knowingly.

Standing next to the big old oak tree, Detective Willow and the apprentice Dixie considered their next move. "Well Dixie, at least we now know what kind of bird it is and they will not be coming back for their egg." said Willow, "So where do we go from here do you think?"

"The Priestess told us to look for the blue pearl to find the answer! What do you suppose she means Detective Willow?" asked Dixie.

"That's right Dixie, I am not sure how the blue pearl will help us, but I guess we may discover the answer once we find it. The question now is, were do we find a blue pearl?"

"Umm! What about the stream, there are a lot of pretty rocks an' things of all colours and shapes there?" said Dixie.

"That's good thinking Dixie, there is always something to be found from the human colonies there. It is a good place to start. Let's go!" said Willow.

With a giggle and swish of Pixie dust, Dixie leaped into the air, looking back to check if Willow was following. He could not see her. Where did she go?

"Right here Dixie!" Willow's laugh came from above. "How did you get up there so fast?" Dixie cried. "I have a little bit of my own magic Dixie. Come on we need to be careful to stay close to the trees to avoid predators." Willow warned.

As they were in the neighbourhood Willow said they would be visiting with the Horidan Dwarf Clan who's village was close by. They always loved to get visits from Willow, who made a point of stopping by any villiages she came close too. King Faidae entrusted her to keep him informed of how the villages where managing.

After the usual greetings, Willow asked the Clans people if anyone knew where they might find a blue pearl. They did not know what a pearl was, but did offer some advice on the likely spots in the stream where a collection of treasures gather. Thanking them, the investigators continued on their journey.

Reaching the stream, they kept a watchful eye on the banks as they slowly flew over the rocks hoping to find the blue round object.

Staying low to the water's edge, they took separate sides to better their chances of seeing something. They came to the site where their friends said the treasures collected, and sure enough there were all sorts of old odds and ends.

"Look, what's that?" cried Dixie, pointing to the edge of the stream where the rocks were layered on the bank. They floated down closer to inspect the object. It was buried in between the rocks and took both of them to tug it out. "No it's not a pearl Dixie." said Willow. Laying it on the pebbles, they inspected the round lid. It's one of those lids the humans seem to lose quite often. She was unable to determine what the lids were made from, certainly not natural, as it comes in all sorts of colours and sizes. Suddenly there was a crack of a branch behind them. Swinging round, Willow and Dixie were confronted by a huge cat with piercing green eyes stalking them.

Willow thought to herself that Dixie would not be quick enough to fly away, as cats are quick and able to jump very high. "Quick Dixie, grab this lid and put it in the water and climb in. I know those cats don't like water so this will be our best chance." Willow said. Pulling the lid to the waters edge, they climbed in, letting the current of the water take them to safety.

"Hey, this is fun." laughed Dixie, as they bobbed up and down with the current of water. The cat followed them from the bank until the bend took them out of sight.

But the water became rougher and Dixie stopped laughing. "Willow, how are we going to get back to the bank?" he asked with a catch in his voice. Willow thought for a moment, knowing they would be unable to fly as the lid was too unstable to stand, and their wings too wet from the splashing water. They will need to come up with a better plan and quickly, as the river was getting wider and the water swells bigger.

Willow opened her satchel to take out her rope. It was made of fine silk, and is very long and light but very strong. She made a loop at one end and said to Dixie, "The next branch we come to I am going to throw the rope over it. I can pull us up to safety, so be ready to grab on to me alright?"

It was not long before they came to a branch that hung over the water. Willow prepared herself to fling the rope over it. "Here we go Dixie, get ready!" called Willow. Dixie held on to Willow as she threw the rope over and grabbed the loop on the other side. The lid began to move away as Willow pulled them slowly upwards. Dixie was looking very nervously at the water below them until finally they were on top of the branch where they rested for a moment. "Phew! That was close." said Dixie. Willow agreed, "It sure was, but we are safe for now. I don't think we will find the blue pearl here Dixie, they actually come from the sea in clams, and I know the humans use them as decoration for their clothes. Maybe we need to go closer to where the humans live to find the blue pearl."

"I know a safe place to look, it's somewhere the little humans go to play on big structures that whirl around and go up and down." declared Dixie, "I go there sometimes to watch them play. They are not so different from us in some things."

"Your right Dixie, they are just bigger than us." Willow said, "Are you ready for a bit of a hike? We will have to walk for a little while, just until our wings dry out enough for us to fly. But we will have to keep a sharp eye out for the cat, he could be anywhere. If we stay close to cover we should be alright."

With a plan in place they traipse through the brush on the forest floor, being careful to stay under the thickest part of the undergrowth that provide them with good cover from prying eyes. They travelled for what seemed like hours, only stopping to check their surrounding. It was not as easy for the Fairy and Pixie to navigate from the ground, as they depend on the horizon from above the trees to get directions.

They came to a clearing where the sun shone golden rays onto a sleeping family of rabbits sunbathing in the warmth. It looked very inviting to Willow and Dixie, as they were becoming very weary. "Let us rest, just a little while?" pleaded Dixie. "Alright, just for a little while. We will stay here on the edge, and if anything comes close the rabbits will hear it before we do and warn us." Resting on their bellies to let the sun shine on their wings, they closed their eyes and drifted off to sleep.

"Willow, Willow wake up, danger coming!" cried out Pipsie rabbit, who had come to warn the little folk of impending danger.

With a start Willow woke and patted Dixie on the shoulder to stir him. "What is it Pipsie, do you know?" asked Willow.

"No, but it's coming fast so we are getting to our burrows to hide. You had better get to safety too!" advised the little rabbit as the thumping noise coming from the otherside of the clearing got closer and closer. "Yes, we will. Go to your family, we will be fine. Our wings have dried enough Dixie, we had better go up." They flew up into the trees to wait to see what was coming through the bush at a fast pace.

The brush began to rustle from the direction of the noise, and out burst Joey with Mrs Roo not too far behind. "They have to be close Mum!" Joey called back. The pair in the tree sighed with relief. "It's Joey and Mrs Roo. Come on Dixie, let's go say hello!" Leaving their hiding place, they flew down to the new arrivals, calling out "Hello there Mrs Roo and Joey, what are you doing so far from home?" Looking up, with relief on their faces, at the sound of Willows voice, Mrs Roo called out, "Oh Detective Willow, we found you at last, we have been looking everywhere. Joey has something very important to tell you."

"What is it? What has happened?" asked Willow. "It's Mr Bower, something terrible has happened. A big old cat has demolished his nest and scattered his decorations all over the place. He is so very upset, as without his nest he won't be able to attract a partner and have babies." Joey cried out.

"Dear Oh dear! Come along Dixie, we will have to help Mr Bower first before we can help Mrs Magpie." said Willow. "We will assist you." said Mrs Roo, "Come along Joey."

The troop of four made their way back to Mr Bower's nest. What they saw was terrible, there was nothing left of it, and all his decorations were scattered everywhere. Mr Bower was huddled in a corner, very dejected and sad, sobbing into his wing. "Mr Bower, are you alright? Don't you worry, we will hep you to fix it up." said Willow. Mr Bower looked up with watery eyes and began to smile. "That is terribly kind of you Willow, I would be ever so grateful. Thank you, thank you all." he said. "Joey and Mrs Roo, can you gather the ornaments while Dixie and I help Mr Bower fix the nest." asked Willow. "Yes of course. Come along Joey, they have been spread far and wide. We can use my pouch to collect them so we can bring them all back here to the nest." said Mrs Roo to Joey.

As everyone worked very hard to set things to right, it was not long before Mr Bower's nest was almost looking good as new. All that remained was to place the blue trinkets Mr Bower had gathered over the summer into their rightful place.

Mrs Roo and Joey had collected them all and put them in a pile near the nest. They each passed an item to Mr Bower so that he could place them where he wanted. It was Dixie who suddenly cried out, "Willow, Willow lookit' here." Holding a large silky smooth round ball in both hands he said, "Is this the blue pearl Willow?"

Willow looked at the trinket in Dixie's hand, turning it over. It glistened so bright and felt so smooth. It certainly looked like a pearl to Willow. Holding it in her hands, a idea began to form in her head. "Yes, yes it is Dixie, well done." she said.

Turning to Mr Bower, Willow asked very delicately. "Mr Bower, isn't it a bit late for you to get a partner for your nest?" "It is now Willow, my time has run out to get offspring this year. But I still wanted to keep my nest looking good, just in case." he said sadly. "Well, if you are willing Mr Bower, I think we can help each other out." Willow explained to Mr Bower about Mrs Magpie's dilemma, and asked if he would take on the bogus egg and raise it as his own. "Oh Willow! Yes, I would very much like to do that, my nest will not go to waste after all. Thank you. Thank you so very much."

With a promise to return that very afternoon with the bogus egg, Willow thanked her helpers for assisting in solving the case. "You have all been very helpful and I could not have solved this one without you. Joey you were a great scout, keep up the good work."

They left Mr Bower fussing over his nest in preparation for the new arrival. Dixie and Willow reached Mrs Magpie's tree, she was still pacing, but when Willow told her the good news she was ever so happy and relieved her babies will once again be safe. "Oh that is wonderful, thank you so much Detective Willow, and of course you Dixie!"

Making sure she got the right egg, Willow emptied her satchel. Making handles from the rope, Willow placed the egg into the bag so that she, and Dixie, can easily carry the egg between them to Mr Bower's nest.

As they reached Mr Bower's nest, they could see he had everything prepared for the new arrival.

They placed the egg under the dome of grass and sticks that covered the nest like a roof. Mr Bower fussed over the egg like it was his very own. He settled himself over the egg to begin the incubation. "Thank you Mr Bower for helping us out." "No, thank you both, you have made me so very happy."

The investigators said a fond farewell to Mr Bower and promised to look in on him every now and again.

On the way back to their home, Willow took Dixie to meet her father, King Faidae. She told her father, the King, of the Cuckoo Bird causing problems in the land, and said that something must be done to re-educate them. The King agreed and said he would speak to them before the next breeding season.

In honor of Dixie's assistance, the King gave him a medal of gold that hung from a silk thread. It was placed over his head by Willow who put a kiss upon his cheek. "You have done very well Dixie, as my apprentice." she said. "It's been great Willow, I can't wait for our next case." Willow laughed and said, "Let's hopefully have a break before launching into another case, alright?"

The pair said goodbye to the King and returned to Willow's home in the tree house. Placing her bag of tools, where she can quickly reach them for the next case, Willow turned to her apprentice and said, "Well Dixie we have had an exciting day. When your medal glows you will know when you are needed, alright?" "Wow, really?" Dixie said looking down at the medal hanging from his neck. "I will come to you right away!" he said faithfully. "Excellent, you had better go home and get some rest too because you will need it. Until next time." said Willow, waving farewell to Dixie as he headed back to his family.

Laying in the hammock with a sigh, Willow said to herself, "Ah! This is the life." She placed her hands under her head as the hammock rocked gently in the breeze. Whispering, "Until next time." she drifted off to sleep with a smile on her lips.

To order additional copies of this book, contact:
Xlibris
1-800-455-039
www.xlibris.com.au
Orders@Xlibris.com.au

ISBN: 978-1-7960-0696-4 (sc)
ISBN: 978-1-7960-0697-1 (e)

Print information available on the last page

Rev. date: 09/27/2019